THE TRONIS ASSIGNMENT

The Assignment Series, Volume 1

E.L. Grover

Published by E.L. Grover, 2022.

This is a work of fiction. Similarities to real people, places, or events are entirely coincidental.

THE TRONIS ASSIGNMENT

First edition. November 8, 2022.

ISBN: 979-8215640753

Written by E.L. Grover.

To my family, who have been beside me in all the ups
and downs.

To the team that inspired Gamma Squadron, though
we have gone separate paths, we are still family.

The tram system made for an interesting ride. John Aerovant had expected the thing to be cobbled together and in need of constant work. Instead, the machine was smooth and almost shiny, with new parts recently brought to Tronis on a ship just like the one he had taken. That, he recalled, was more like he expected: tight, claustrophobic, and full of unpleasant smells.

John had spent the first three hyperspace jumps from Earth in his cabin. The next four, he spent upfront, flexing his media credentials to get footage and interviews from the trip for his story. He rightly figured the transport crew kept their section of the ship clear of the smell of tightly crammed people and machine parts.

The conversations started out as just for show, but he became interested when they spoke about the recent pirate raids near their destination. Tronis was a colony on what most, on Earth, called the mid-frontier. It was established and growing but wasn't new, having been settled fifty years prior.

They had missed out on most of the Earth-Shezlan war, being in an out of the way area. Most of the fighting had occurred around Earth and the colonies close to the Shezlan's boarder. This meant that when Earth needed resources from off world, Tronis was ready with supplies. Trade boomed and the colony became the up-and-coming new world.

This came with trouble as the trade route itself was absent dedicated patrols. Opportunistic elements decided it was worth the risk to make some extra money. The Tronis government had limited resources and was unable to do much. The United Nations Space Corps was still recovering from the war and was still being organized into something more than a haphazard military. Consequently, the raiders flourished, eventually getting too bold.

"I hear they take prisoners for sport these days," one of the crew said.

John doubted it. They were just people looking to make some easy money, not psychopaths who had a need to kill for sport. At least he hoped that was the case.

"Why aren't you and the others more worried about them attacking this ship? I mean, we have passengers and some expensive equipment on here," John said.

"The cruiser they are sending to Tronis, the Australia."

John nodded. "I had heard they were sending military forces. I just didn't think it'd be a cruiser. I figured one of the fast attack ships or a destroyer group."

The tram's whistle brought him out of his musing. His stop was coming up, so he grabbed his bag and tablet. Moving to the door, he smiled at the few passengers left then hopped off.

He took his first real look at Tronis. Prefabbed buildings along rugged streets. A majority were repurposed cargo containers from the first landings. Designed to be sturdy and stacked together, they were a common sight in any colony world. John looked over the clever painting to differentiate them from each other. Some had large murals dedicated to the first colonists. Some had advertising for products and work.

He smiled. The place felt homey until he noticed the people. They were moving around, going in and out of the stores, some with bundles, some without, but all had their heads down, their coats pulled tight to their bodies. He said hello to passersby as he walked, only to receive a suspicious glare in response. The people made the air feel heavy.

He took a few videos and photos to document the situation. The footage would be important, and he wanted his viewers to feel this as he had just now. Once that was done, he started to locate his actual targets: Gamma Squadron, the United Nations Space Corps Special Forces team he heard was going to be here.

He had worked with them before, documenting their actions during some terrorist incidents back on Earth. They had been called in to secure the safety of the African Unification Conference a year before. The UN Military and his news agency thought it would be good to have some public stories about their efforts.

The team, on the other hand, was not impressed with the idea. John had spent many of his conversations receiving clipped yes and no answers. Even open questions got shut down as they would either just stare at him or counter with their own. He was used to that from many years of interviewing, but the members of this unit had it down to an art.

There were exceptions, of course. The Chief Petty Officer, Eric Keith, was at least willing to expand on things. He had also warned John how bad the interviews would go until the team felt he was safe to speak with. Just because someone in command said he was alright, didn't mean he really was. They had to trust his character first.

The team's commander said much the same thing and made the visual action of being seen talking to John. That helped some, but most were still very leery. He was sure they were not going to be impressed to see him here. That was too bad, though. He had a story to get, and he had his own desires as well.

John imagined some of the team running to catch stores and some oddities like other tourists, laughing to himself as he walked. They were surprisingly human when not on a mission or training. Although, with the way everyone was looking at him, he doubted they would be doing anything of the sort. They would have found a bar that was quiet and willing to tolerate their presence.

There was only one he felt fit the bill, and after some hunting, he managed to locate it. As it was evening, he figured his chances were pretty good he'd find them.

The bar in question had a dim sign flashing in the evening's glow. A slight mist settled into the air; the locals said it was common. The night's fog made for an amazing sunset, but he wasn't here to see that. The building, made of polymers and reinforced steel, looked to have been built after the first landings.

He looked around and quickly noticed the team sitting in the back corner playing cards and laughing. He could see empty beer pitchers as well. The rest of the bar was nice, tall tables and games scattered around. People sat and drank, laughed and played. Some music played that he wasn't totally sure he liked. Something with heavy drumbeats and yelling.

He moved to the counter and nodded to the brown-haired woman behind it. "Can I get three pitchers of whatever they are drinking?" he asked and pointed toward the back.

She looked over and frowned. "Ah, the soldiers. Been in here every few days this week, playing cards and drinking booze."

"Work hard, play hard?" he asked with a chuckle.

She shrugged and gathered the pitchers, setting them on the wooden countertop. John ran his fingers over it as she worked. "This is really nice. Why use it as a bar top?"

The woman smiled and knocked on it. "Real wood from Earth. My family's place. Years back, they renovated a pool hall. Used the wood that could be salvaged from the old tables to make the bar counters. I took some of it when we came here. Gives me a connection to home, you know?"

He nodded and smiled. "I see." He rubbed his hand on the lacquered finish. It felt old and cared for. He pulled out his tablet and made a few notes as she stepped over with the pitchers ready to go.

"What's that then?" She asked, motioning to what he was working on.

"Notes. I'm a journalist that's following a story to do with those soldiers over there. Your bar top here is something I want to remember about this place. It has its own story."

The woman nodded, "That's sweet." She pointed to the beer. "Good luck talking to them. They aren't bad customers, but they are not friendly. Couple of locals tried to pick a fight last time."

John nodded. "I'll keep that in mind. Maybe a peace offering will help?"

He chuckled as the bartender gave him a funny look and moved off to get back to work. John knew not to go directly to the table. That was asking to challenge them. The one beside them, however, was at least a safer bet. One of the team recognized instantly him, and, of course, it had to be the largest one. The man stood out, even around the team.

Tall and very dark-skinned, the man's accent was unusually thick. He was one of the team that took the African assignment personally. Turns out he had grown up in some of the more unpleasant places and had the stories to back it up. John never doubted the things he said he had experienced, and it let him understand why he was so hard to talk to.

"What the fuck? How did you get here, Newsie?"

John smiled. "Well, there are these things called transport shuttles, I rode one of those out here just to see your smiling face, Bekele."

"No one likes a smart ass," Bekele said, his deep tones reverberating all around the room despite the music.

"That's why I'm a wiseass," John replied.

He noticed the rest had turned to see what all the fuss was about. He recognized most of the faces. There were a couple new ones. He greeted them with a wave and a motion to the beer.

"I figured I would try to be nice this time and offer the drinks before I tried to pick your brains."

Most of the team went back to playing their card game, even Bekele, who John had never seen turn down free booze. John figured he would try again with someone he knew would speak civilly. He looked around and couldn't find him, though.

"Where's Keith?"

This time the answer came from another he knew, Eversley. He was about the fittest one on the team near as John could tell. Despite the copious amount of bar food sitting on the plate in front of him. The man had two vices John knew of, one of which was the pizza rolls sitting on the plate. The man's accent was hard to place, but John figured he was safe saying some place in the middle of America.

"He's with the bigwigs. Good luck getting in that conversation."

"Kinda like this one?"

The reply was just an extended middle finger.

John rubbed his face, if it were possible to get worse, these people had. He considered what other ways he could gain an inroad. There was going to the command staff here and practically making them do it. He ruled that out as fast as he thought it up.

"Whose this?" came a female voice beside him.

John turned, surprised he had missed her approach. She was shorter than him, brown hair that was perhaps shoulder length but kept orderly. She was attractive, sharp eyes and a cute nose. He smiled and extended his hand.

"Hello, John Aerovant, Earth News Net."

She shook his hand after a moment's consideration, "Jackie Silverling, UNSC"

"That's Newsie," came Eversley's voice.

She smiled and nodded after releasing his hand. "Ah. Well. This should be interesting. Good luck."

"Thanks?"

She moved to the table and John had to force himself to remember why he was there. Then a look at the table and the faces turned towards him, told him enough. The next couple of weeks were going to be rough. They would see to that.

"It'll get better, Newsie," came another voice behind him.

John turned and saw a blond woman walking towards him from the same direction Silverling had. He smiled and nodded, extending his hand. She shook it and looked between him and the group at the table.

"Hello again, Sasha. Like the haircut."

She had cropped her hair since he last seen her, going from a pixie cut to this more masculine, near buzzed look. Her hair was just long enough she would need a comb to make it functional. It had the advantage of allowing the blond in her hair to be more prominent, he thought. When she had it longer, there were some brown highlights. This suited her better.

"Well thanks, Newsie. Holte by the way," she said before looking at him again. "Give them time. I'll maybe put in a good word or two. Keith's at the base if you want to catch him."

John nodded, "Yeah. I'll see you later."

CHIEF PETTY OFFICER Keith walked through the doors of the Colonial Defense Office. The lobby was not unlike any he had seen before. Sterile looking, a large oval counter desk, some modern art, a pair of elevator doors behind the desk, and a group of impressive looking men in suits and sunglasses.

Pretending to look tough, of course.

"I have a meeting with Colonial Director Hawthorn," he said with his best smile as he presented his ID.

The man behind the desk looked at him with a mostly bored expression. He was clearly over the show his boss was putting up. "Your commander was here twenty-five minutes ago."

Keith nodded. "I expected he would. Gives him and the Director time to sort things. Then I can arrive and get to work."

"Lots of experience with politicians?"

Keith shrugged. "Politicians, commanding officers, news reporters, ex-girlfriends, they all require a careful touch."

That drew a chuckle as the man opened the door. "Well, good luck then."

"Thanks."

The ride up was peaceful. The last couple of days had been a serious headache, especially with the arrival of Newsie. His team was on edge with the guy following them the last few days. He had spoken with Newsie and said he'd do his best to talk them into being cooperative, but ultimately, it was up to him to gain ground with the team.

The ding of the elevator interrupted his thoughts. As expected, the same sort of men in suits met him. There was also the addition of a dark-haired woman in a business suit. She extended her hand as he stepped off the elevator. He detected a scent of sandalwood and some sort of berry.

"Chief Petty Officer Keith, I'm Assistant Colonial Director Alice Ball," she said.

He nodded and extended his hand. "Good to meet you."

"This way please, the Director and Commander Jubert are still having their initial meeting."

Keith nodded. "I see. How's it going in there?"

She made a face but didn't say anything right away. Instead, she led him down the hall and past several pieces of art and a window looking over a large section of the colony. She stopped and faced him.

"Chief Petty Officer Keith, how much do you know about our colony?"

"First off, Keith is fine. I hardly answer to my first name since joining the military, and it seems like a mouthful for you to say my rank," he countered.

"Mister Keith then."

He nodded. That was likely as good as it would get. "Tronis was settled by Great Brittan in twenty-one eleven, if I recall."

She nodded and he continued, "The colony was generally considered to be a failure in its first ten years. Population issues alongside of poor resource production meant few returns for the founding nation's efforts. That all changed with the discovery of valuable material in the system's asteroids."

"That's correct. The trade agreements Earth made during first contact with the Zindri Commerce Agency were almost exclusively for the ore we found."

"I had heard there was a large amount of zecreitium discovered."

There was pride in her smile and voice. "Indeed. The only issue," her voice took an edge, "was that we didn't have the resources to process it. So, it still had to be sent back to Earth."

He nodded. That was the real issue most colonies had with Earth. They didn't have the resources or infrastructure for refinement of the ore. The ZCA was picky about the quality of the refined ore. They would pay well for the unrefined ore, but if Earth could provide the refined product, so much the better.

There were also the manufacturing needs of Earth. Anything with artificial gravity needed zecreitium to be refined properly. The material had to be refined to a specific structural state and charged with energy to generate gravity. Earth's refineries were currently the only ones able to meet those needs, primarily as they were provided by the ZCA.

"Well, I doubt it will take long for Tronis to get refineries equal to Earth."

She nodded, "That's part of the issue. People here know that this colony can be fully self-sufficient, and with work, able to compete with Earth in the market. They feel that us bringing the military here is a mistake, and something that will end up setting us back."

He nodded. "A lot of colonies get that mind set. Seeing us as the bully come to enforce the rules."

"Please understand, I am not of that mindset. The situation here is beyond what we can manage. I know this. So does Director Hawthorne."

"But?"

"There are political opponents using this to garner support and weaken our position. Not to mention the protests that will occur soon."

"Anything we should be concerned about?"

She shook her head. "Not yet. Just expect the crowds and yelling."

"A real win with the recovery of the hostages would make them look kind of foolish."

"It would, and it's not just for that reason. I hope your mission goes well. I worry about the people taken. It just happens to also serve my position in keeping the peace between people here easier if they are saved."

An aid arrived and derailed further discussion, saying that the Director and the Commander was waiting for them both. After a short trip, they entered the main conference room of the building. Dominated by a large wooden table and office chairs. The rest of the cream-colored room had a few pictures of the colony on the wall.

Commander Jubert and the Director were getting along well enough. Both men were chuckling at some joke or another. After introductions, he took his seat, the lights dimmed, and a holographic projection of the Tronis system appeared above the table.

Captain Jubert led the discussion. "About four hours ago, a signal from one of Tronis' defense ships stated they had tracked a lone pirate raider to this area here."

The hologram focused on a moon of the fourth planet from the sun, on the opposite side of the star from Tronis itself. Moon was too strong a word; it appeared to be nothing but fragments and debris. Though at its core there was a substantial sized section.

"Rather out of the way to be anything other than its base of operations," Keith commented.

Jubert nodded. "That's my assessment, as well as that of the defense force."

Keith nodded. "I don't suppose they have mapped this debris field in a while?"

Director Hawthorn shook his head. The man was probably in his late sixties and looked to be in good health. "The last time we had any work, there was an initial mining agency about ten years ago. It's been abandoned for the last eight."

"Wonderful," Keith muttered.

"I've spoken with the CO of the Australia, and he thinks she can get through. So, the plan is to send a lander from the Australia. Once clear of the field, we will proceed with an attack on their base, starting with whatever landing site they have. From there, we will create a command post and infiltrate the base, effecting a hostage rescue," Commander Jubert explained.

Director Hawthorn interrupted. "I'd like some sort of presence from Tronis' defense force. This is a local matter, and they should be involved in some degree."

"I'm not taking anyone in with my team on the ground," Keith said.

The Assistant Director shot him a look, as did the Director. Commander Jubert simply nodded; he clearly had expected resistance on the matter. Keith held his hand up a moment, trying to get ahead of the impending arguments.

"Here is my reasoning. We are a team trained to work together on our own. No offense to your defense force. I am sure they are committed but they simply aren't up to par with my team. That will hamper coordination and put the hostages at risk."

"There is another option," Jubert offered. "the colony has a small squadron of attack craft, yes? They will be used to provide cover for the landing. Clearing out the landing bay of any threat to the team. They can also make sure none of the pirates try to escape."

Keith was glad to see a nod come from the director and his assistant on the matter. The rest of the meeting went about how he expected, discussing known hostage numbers and how long the military would remain after the recovery. All the things that made the world go round, and as far as Keith was concerned, made it difficult to do his job.

Thankfully, it was over quickly as they obviously had to get to work. The car ride to the base was quiet at first. Then Jubert broke the silence.

"Stomped on the man's feet pretty hard back there, Keith."

"I know. I just can't shake it. Last thing I wanted was some inexperienced halfwit putting my people at risk again."

"They are my people too. Don't forget that."

"Again, I know. It's just going to be busy enough with Newsie running around. I'm not sending someone home in a box again."

"This is the wrong line of work for that thought. No matter how hard we train, how many hours you put in, the chance of not bringing them all home is always there."

"True, but I can at least mitigate it and having a team of colonial defense force weekend warriors isn't my idea of being careful."

"That's probably a little harsh."

"Maybe, but I've already got one extra to keep tabs on."

"You could make him stay back too, you know."

"You going to explain that to his dad? Admiral Aerovant?"

Jubert laughed at that, then shook his head. "No, I don't think I'd like to."

"See? I'll pick the battle I know I can win, thank you."

They lapsed back into silence again. Keith watched the city move past the windows, wondering briefly if what he and Assistant Director Ball had discussed was true. Tronis had the chance to become the premier colony and a force of its own. Many worlds were on the verge. They just lacked Earth's infrastructure. That took time to build. It wasn't just people and resources, it was quality education and engineers. For some reason, they all seemed to resent that about Earth.

"Keith?" Commander Jubert's voice brought him back to the here and now.

"What's up?"

"Just got word from the Australia's CO to meet the intercept and get us on target in the best time. We depart in two hours. Get the squads ready."

Keith nodded, pulling out his tablet. He typed in two words, 'Roll out.'

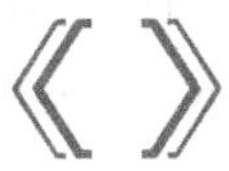

THE CABIN AREA OF THE drop ship felt claustrophobic. Uncomfortably so, according to John. The space between the aisles was just wide enough to walk through. He looked up and down the row of operators as he tried to find a place to sit. They weren't rude about it, but he got that impression when he needed to wait.

The operators tolerated him more than they used to. They didn't separate him using seating this time. The only empty seats belonged to Commander Jubert and Chief Keith. Before, empty seats made space between him and the rest of the team.

Not that it changed anything. He was still a tag-along. This time, his escort was the team's newest member, Jonathon Andrews. The new replacements always got the lousy details. Here, the 'shit job' was keeping track of a journalist while on the ground—not that John made it difficult.

He powered up his tablet and keyed the drone camera. The drone was new, and he still had to experiment with it. John noticed it was a modified version of current military surveillance models. The idea was to be used during a mission and not draw attention to him trying to record. He lifted the drone in his free hand, palm up. It took a moment, but then it lifted and balanced in the air. While it calibrated, he turned on the record function and directed it to buzz through the interior cabin, so he got better images of the team. It flew off on its own, and he fiddled with his stylus before starting this trip's log.

Holte was reading over his shoulder. She gave him a thump. "Telling all our secrets again, Newsie?"

"Naw, I figured I'd save that for some exposé on excessive force and military spending."

Holte laughed and sat in the jump seat across from him. "We will be asking for all your toys back right after it drops."

"Ha-ha."

She smiled in return and shrugged. "Why would anyone want to go into a firefight without a weapon? What made you want to do this?" she asked.

He looked up and then past her. "Why did you quit playing baseball? I heard you had a locked in contract for some serious money as a catcher."

"I wanted to serve."

"Right off the recruiting poster?" He quirked an eyebrow. "Well, even if that's the case, I suppose it fits mine. I want to serve, but I didn't want to be in one of the military branches. I got enough of that life with my father. So, in place of that, I serve by telling the whole of what occurred. Here, I'm not writing about the United Nations Security Council sending troops to secure a trade route, I'm telling the story of the men and women who are sent to do it."

"I suppose that gives you a small pass for asking us so many questions," she said with a grin.

John looked up and spun his stylus in his fingers. "Good. Cause I've got a few. Aren't you folks kind of overkill for hostage rescue from some local pirates?"

Holte shook her head. "Not in this case. The Tronis colony director has been trying to deal with it for a few months now. So, trade being strangled back to Earth, and a sixth cargo vessel being taken makes it time to step up. Plus, have you seen what has been done to the people recovered from those attacks?"

John winced and his stomach churned a bit. Her question brought to mind the first sights he saw on this assignment.

He was with Andrews getting some shots of the spaceport and workers when the recovery ship came in. John insisted on getting some shots. Andrews told him he really didn't want to. John just shrugged him off and moved into the makeshift infirmary it had landed in.

By the time he got there, they had people moved into the medical area, and all the rest went to the morgue. John, in a spectacular lack of sense, slipped out of Andrews' leash again. He made about three steps into the tent. The smell hit him as he entered—that disinfectant smell mixed with remains. His first instinct was to gasp for breath, and, against his better judgment, he did.

His eyes darted about, seeing people placed on the floor. No tarps had been laid over them yet. People had been exposed to the hard vacuum of space. Some were clearly shot by energy weapons without any protective gear. Still, others had been bound and executed. He could still see the cable wrapped around their hands and feet.

When he saw the people in medical gowns and masks moving about with clipboards and cameras, he left, trying to get outside and someplace private before he puked. He made it to the rail of the dock instead, retching over and over until he dry heaved. Andrews patted his shoulder, telling him to slow down and breathe.

The interviews with the survivors were almost as terrible. The sight of their wounds, the state they were in—John was sure he would never forget that. The stories they told only made the things he saw before worse. People had been shoved into the airlocks, and the external doors opened. Others had been lined up and executed.

John looked at Holte. "I have sadly," he replied.

Holte nodded as a soft expression flashed across her face. "You're a good guy, Newsie. Most people tend to think journalists are worms, if I'm being honest."

"Thanks for that. I think. That means you won't stab me for asking Silverling for a drink one of these nights?"

"You never have to worry about me stabbing you," she retorted. "That's Granberg's job."

John looked over and swallowed hard. The man in question was currently bent over, working a whetstone over the blade of a hand axe. His tan skin glistened lightly with perspiration, and he was sure, given the fresh shave on Granberg's head, the man shaved with it. John's eyes kept going back to the axe, a perk of the special operations teams. Custom gear was more prevalent, so long as it met UNSC guidelines—but who picks an axe?

"Yeah. I don't think stab is the right word there," he replied.

"Who is getting stabbed now?" asked Keith as he dropped into the vacant seat.

John almost jumped. The chief petty officer was probably six inches taller than Holte. For a Texas giant, he moved with surprising silence. John hadn't noticed him come down the ladder.

"Newsie here," Holte replied with a grin, "wants to ask Pew-Pew on a date."

"Hey, now, I just said drinks!"

Both operators laughed, Keith even giving John a thump on the shoulder. He tried to take it in stride. The way they laughed was a good sign. The team had some dark humor in it, which could make it difficult to feel welcome. As he saw it, this was a start, at least.

"So, Keith, what do you think we need to do about that?" Holte asked.

"I'm thinking feeding him to Bekele might be more entertaining."

"You two are a riot. You know that? You ever going to stop calling me Newsie?" he asked. Both shook their heads; nicknames tended to stick on the team. It was part of a rite of passage that they were putting him through. It would take time, like most things. In a way, John felt he should be grateful. They were far rougher on operators who joined the team. John shifted as the chief kneeled in the space between them and the others. He gave a thump to the side of Granberg as a greeting, receiving a grunt in reply. John's attention was soon drawn to Bekele, the large man telling a story.

The man was always bragging. This time was no different. He was talking about where he went for beers the night before. What women they saw, whose bed he slept in. That he was married was a footnote. John thought about going over and testing how accepted he had been. A quick look at Granberg's axe discouraged that. Instead, he toggled the camera to fly over and film.

"I think I'm going to chat with the flight team and see about getting some good external shots of the Australia as we depart," John said.

Holte nodded and smirked. Then her eyes widened. "Oh! Ask them to show you her battle scars."

John looked back, confused. "What?"

Holte nodded. "Her battle scars from the Earth Shezlan War. They never replaced the ventral armor plates. You'll see them as we drop free."

"That was fifty years ago! How are they not fixed?"

Holte just shrugged. "Hard to say. Thought it'd make for good stuff for your story. Don't ya know?"

John chuckled. Holte's Minnesota accent poked through every so often. It was amusing and almost attractive. She had shot him down early, though. Given what he'd seen, he figured it wasn't personal. He had the wrong equipment, and he had the decency not to smile too wide at it. Then he heard the others raise their voices.

He noticed the large man, Bekele, was evidently getting to what he considered the 'Good part' of his story. John stood and watched, unable to ignore the unfolding event.

"Was she at least human this time?" Keith asked.

Bekele looked indignant as the others all started laughing. He joined in after a moment.

The man's bass laugh rattled ears. "You just jealous you're so ordinary, Keith!"

"Oh, that what it is? Being 'exotic' is your trade secret?"

"Sure! You ask Granberg—he knows!"

Granberg held his hands up. "Hey, leave me out of this!"

Keith was laughing too hard to retort, so Eversley covered for him. "Fuck too! At least he's from the Mediterranean! Guys and gals from there are supposed to be exotic."

"Hey! Africa is exotic!" Bekele shot back.

"If you say so," Eversley replied.

"We going to start poking at where people are from?" Qureshi rolled her prayer rug as she stood. Her rug rolled tight, she placed it in a protective tube and slid it under her seat. The look she gave the rest of them was prim and proper as she tightened her hijab.

"We weren't too loud, were we?" Keith asked, his tone serious again.

"No. I was finished before the laughing started. Though, I thank you for interrupting the conquest before it got graphic," Qureshi said.

Keith shot Bekele a withering look. The large man's grin vanished as he bobbed his head.

"Sorry, Q," he managed in his quietest voice.

She waved it off. "Allah is forgiving. I may not be."

Eversley looked at the woman and then back to Bekele. "I think that's her way of saying, 'Don't do it again, dude.'"

John checked his watch and noticed the time—prayer time. The first lesson he had learned about Gamma Squadron was the way the team reacted if anyone bothered Qureshi during prayer. Once John saw some port workers at the colony stop and start making passes at the woman at the park. The whole squadron had been out for a run and warm-up at the large park and took a break so she could conduct her prayers.

John had been sitting off to the side at a table and bench, studying his EV suit manual. By the time he had stood to say something, half the team had returned. They promptly moved between her and the workers, making it very clear what would happen if they persisted. John remembered thinking to cue up his camera, but decided not to. People were already touchy about United Nations Space Corps being in the colony. He had no intention of making the divide worse.

Thankfully, they got the point and moved on. Between Eversley, Granberg, and Bekele, there was no doubt it would have turned ugly. Qureshi finished her prayers and got up to rejoin the workouts. No words were exchanged about it. the following days, Eversley had stayed behind while Qureshi prayed.

John smiled and then slipped into the cabin with the flight crew, pausing long enough to let the commander pass. Mountains took up less space and were more movable. Once he got into the cabin, John sat in the observation seat. One of the pilots looked over and nodded.

"You're the one they call Newsie, right? Gonna make us famous?" the man asked.

John laughed and shrugged. "I might, depends on how cool you make my tour."

The other pilot laughed but didn't look up. She was watching the debris field they were navigating through. Her intensity caught John's attention. He pointed to her. "What's she doing?"

"Making sure these ancient bits of moon don't kill us," he explained.

"That's comforting," John said.

The woman tilted her head, but her eyes were glued to the readouts. "It's not as bad as it sounds. These bits follow the same path they always have. What ever happened to this moon some million years ago just tossed all this junk out here in the void, drifting in orbit still, so it's all haphazard. If I'm not watching, a chunk could come and slam into us. This little drop ship won't take the abuse the Australia can."

"Sounds like a lousy place to run and hide. You'd die getting to it."

"Naw," the male pilot replied. "The pirates have gotten the whole field mapped, know the path of every rock out here. For the pirates, it's just a quick trip. Name's Jaw-Jack, by the way. This is Thump."

John extended his hand. "John Aerovant. Earth News Net. Jaw-Jack and Thump? How'd you two get those call signs?"

John suspected that pilots got their call signs from some antic or another that stood out to their compatriots. Seldom was it anything cool. He could guess what Jaw-Jack had been doing. Thump made him nervous. The first thing that came to mind was a bad landing. Instead of a graceful touch down, she likely hit the ground all at once.

"It's all good. I haven't done it since my first month," she said.

John nodded. "How long have you been flying?"

"A month."

John's retort was cut off as a shadow fell over the flight cabin. He looked out into the void and saw the Australia passing over head. They were about to clear the field, and the cruiser would be there to absorb the incoming fire while shielding the drop ship's deployment. John's eyes went to see the scars. There on the underside of the ship were a pair of deep gouges and melted points.

"Holy shit, those are massive," John said in awe.

"Got that right. Phalanx Class cruiser. Toughest ship in the Fleet and the scars to prove it!" Jaw-Jack said. "So, the story goes that a force of a dozen Shezlan ships were making an attack run for the Lunar Colony. The Australia and her escorts were tasked with the defense. The Shezlan tried to blitz the line and just run past them. Held fire till they were almost point blank."

Thump jumped in. "Meant there was no room to move to try to get clear, but the commander of the Australia saw it coming and ordered the helmsmen to light up all the ventral thrusters and execute a tight turn."

John nodded, picking up on the idea. "She raised the ship and turned it around, so the Shezlan would pass under them. Also, the Australia would be turned and able to hit them with a broadside."

"Pretty slick, eh?" asked Thump, her eyes still glued to the screens. John looked up at the gouges in the hull again. "Yes, indeed. May have to do a deep dive on the Australia and crew someday."

"Hey, us first," Jaw-Jack added.

John laughed, thinking it was strange the pilots would be more willing to chat him up. Then again, they didn't have to worry about him being in their business all the time. He nodded to Jaw-Jack and agreed. "Yes, you and those on this mission first."

"Tiger Sharks coming over now. Here we go," Thump said.

The attack craft accelerated past them. They reminded him of attack helicopters he had seen in the air and space museums: a narrow frame, slight wings holding weapon pods. A gun that could swivel under the nose. He thought maybe they weren't as long. He snapped a few photos with his tablet and was looking them over when a beep drew his attention. His heart rate increased and had to take several deep breaths to keep his appearance of calm. John figured he might have been okay if it weren't for how quiet Jaw-Jack got when he turned.

"Signal from Australia. They are releasing us from the dock field," Thump called out.

The two pilots went to work. They spoke back and forth about telemetry, rocks, and speed. He felt comfortable that they worked so well together. Each talked quickly and calmly. Thump flipped a switch, changing the lights in the ship to a dark red. His heart rate came back up.

"We have visual if you want to look," Thump said over her shoulder.

John took a breath and stood, moving forward, so he could see out the cockpit window. There, amid the ever-circling debris field, was the remains of the moon itself. The heads-up display on the window showed an indicator in blue. It read 'Objective' in small, neat print, then several red dots appeared.

Before he could ask, Jaw-Jack had already put a hand on his forearm. "Hey, Newsie, you might want to go sit down and get strapped in. The base is there on the moon, and they've got defenses."

John felt a tingly feeling in the pit of his stomach. After a second look, he turned and made his way back to his seat. He was just settling in and getting his helmet located when he saw Keith and Commander Jubert looking at a tablet. Before he could ask, Keith jumped up.

"Thirty seconds!" he barked.

The words caused an instant reaction. Helmets went on almost at the same moment—except for John's as he was slow at it. He still had to methodically secure the helmet and pressurize his suit. The Mark II combat suit was self-contained for potential zero atmosphere operations, but that depended on the operator doing it right. Something John wanted to be very sure he did.

"You need to get faster at that," Holte said flatly.

He nodded. "I know. I just can't help but want to double check it all. I don't know how you trust these things so much."

She shrugged. "Few hundred hours of training and making mistakes. Just be sure the ones you make aren't your last."

He nodded, and before he could add more to the conversation, the commander spoke up. "Mouths shut, ears open! Just like we planned. We secure the hangar, then the hangar control room. From there, first squad moves through the compound to the hostages. No detours. Second squad will engage the armory and barracks areas. Once we have the hostages, first squad calls out 'Romeo' and falls back to the hangar, followed by second squad. Then we evac and blow this place to hell."

The chorus of 'Yes, sir!' rattled over the internal comms of the suits. John took the moment to recover his drone and then tied into the ship's battle network. He could keep tabs on what was going on outside the ship easily that way. The whole network between the Australia, Tiger Sharks, and the drop ship was nearly instant. The ship accelerated and John wondered about the rocks and what the pilots meant about defenders. His mouth felt dry as he looked up at Holte, who winked at him.

"Here we go," Keith said to him over the com. "You do what my people say, and you'll get through just fine."

JASON 'BLACKOUT' MITCHELL shifted in his seat. Tiger Sharks were a comfortable craft to fly, but combat always made him wish for a better seat. He glanced at the screens and his heads-up display, taking in the data as the pirate's base came into view. The time was now, and they were about to fly into the fire.

"Blackout to Worm and Smokes. Weapons hot!" he called over the coms.

Worm called back first, her voice smooth and controlled. "Copy Blackout. Weapons hot. I've got three ships moving to intercept the Australia."

"Smokes here, can confirm. Also copy weapons hot. Looks like the Australia is gonna get the first kill of the day." His voice was a bit more animated, but he was still confident and in control.

There was a surprising amount of disappointment in Smoke's tone. As fighter pilots, they wanted to be at the tip of the spear, getting those first kills and clearing the way. That's just not how it worked this time, though.

"Copy that," he replied and looked up out of his cockpit window. He saw the Australia clearly, looming over the open space between the large mountain-sized chunks of debris that remained of the moon. Then he saw the trio of ships Worm had pointed out. He shook his head. They were heading straight at the Australia. For just a moment, he caught himself feeling sorry for them.

As he watched all three of the pirate ships opened fire, he saw the glow of plasma and the telltale yellow streak of hot ballistic rounds—far too soon. They must have been panicking in those little crafts. The plasma rounds broke down before reaching their target. Meant for close range engagement, plasma diffused quickly, the particles breaking down as they moved through the cold void of space.

Smokes came over the coms. "Welp, that's gonna be a quick fight."

"Agreed," came Worm in response. "I doubt the ballistics even scratched the paint on the forward armor."

Jason smirked but still cued his com up. "Alright, cut the chatter. Watch for anyone deciding to run."

Despite his order, he wanted to cheer when he saw the Australia return fire. Six gauss cannons aligned along the hull fired at once, sending four-foot-long projectiles at Mach 33. The small tendrils of cooling gas still clinging to the rounds on exiting their targets made a ghostly sight as they drew a small thin line against the blackness of space, connecting two of the pirate ships for just an instant.

Jason knew both crafts were suffering violent decompression. The rounds would have torn gaping holes in the armor upon entry and exit. The atmosphere would rush out, and the sheer force of the projectile's passing would be pulling everything out with it. Each twisted hulk hung in the void, a slight turn imparted by the rounds that passed through them.

"Runner! Runner! Runner!" came Worm's voice over the comms.

Jason looked to his radar and noted the blip identified as a pirate attack ship. It was speeding away from the Australia, trying to run for the debris field. He quickly tapped the keys and noted the course; they'd pass above them. An idea came to mind. "Copy that, wedge formation! Burn your aft dorsal and forward ventral thrusters. We'll stay moving forward but change our gun angles," he said.

"If he makes that field, he's gone! We can't keep up with him there!" Smokes said.

Jason shook his head. He knew that, and so did anyone else who thought about it. He resisted the urge to call him on it, though. The tense nature of battle sometimes had the man thinking out loud. Maybe all of them were guilty of it—at least from time to time. He shook his head to clear the errant thoughts. His thumb hung over the large red button on his flight control. All the moisture was gone from his mouth as he waited for the pirate ship to pass into his firing arch. "Just a bit more," he whispered to himself.

He was rewarded with a hum from the computer, telling him he had a target lock. "Light 'em up!" he called.

All three Tiger Sharks opened fire in unison with mini-guns, throwing one-foot-long rods of steel through the void. Though not at the speed of the gauss cannons on the Australia, they moved fast enough to have the force needed to obliterate the armor of the pirate's craft. Also, with no concern for what was beyond the target, each ship could fire without care. The rounds would carry into the field and smash into the asteroids.

Everyone was on the mark as the rounds struck the pirate ship. It exploded as its hull was breached in the torrent of fire from all three Tiger Sharks. The fireball was massive, the force of the blast and flames from combusted fuel not being restricted by atmosphere as it threw shrapnel and the remains of the crew in all directions, leaving them to float and twist in the void.

"Target down," Jason said over the com. "Reform. Let's get to the hangar before they try to air anymore."

All three of them changed their orientation and moved forward. Jason noted the warning alarm as the surface air defenses for the base started to track them. While their armor was good, it could not stand up to weapons designed to take out such craft. Jason swore before getting on the com.

"Spread out and go evasive! Air defense systems on the surface of the objective!" he said.

The hail of rounds coming from the surface guns appeared to be solid lines, so many rounds were being fired. They zipped back and forth, attempting to pin the Tiger Sharks down and inflict damage. Jason kept his ship tumbling and turning, his part in this deadly dance. He relaxed and let his instinct and training do the work, keeping his mind silent.

"Australia, fire control to all Tiger Sharks. Laser mark the guns, so we can clear your way!" It was the call he'd been waiting for.

The slightest motion from his fingers brought up the target designator, marking the target for the Australia's big guns. He and the others couldn't spare the attention for much more than that. No callouts or quips, just the hum of the laser designator.

After what felt like an eternity, the rounds from the Australia streaked across his field of view and hit the surface guns. Each position got two rounds, just to be sure everyone was dead or running. The force of the impacts sent debris high off the surface that just hung in the void.

"Nice shooting!" he said over the com. "Alright, Worm, Smokes, on me. Let's get that hangar cleared!"

Jason led the Tiger Sharks in a twisting turn, counter to the rotation of the large chunk of moon that housed the pirate base. Soon enough, the hangar came into view, and the Tiger Sharks ignited their front thrusters and came to a halt just outside the hangar.

"Two enemy attack craft are in take off!" came Worm's voice.

"Copy that! Fire at will!" Jason responded, depressing the fire button on his flight control.

He smiled just a bit as he watched the rounds from all three Tiger Sharks penetrate the pirate ships. They both fell back to the flight deck and exploded, the fire looking like liquid as it splashed over the flight crews and various equipment on the deck. Hard pieces of debris were tossed in all directions, adding to the chaos.

In the same instant, he started to sweep the minigun back and forth, spraying death at anything that could potentially be hiding something. As one trio of people ran for the door to the compound, he swung the minigun in position and fired. All three disappeared in a mist as the sheer force of the rounds passing through them shattered their bodies. Jason cringed a slight bit; that was certainly not a way he ever wanted to go.

"Anyone see anything?" he asked over the com. "Nothing here," Worm replied.

"Nadda," said Smokes.

"Copy that," Jason replied, and then he tapped the open channel to the ship carrying Gamma Squadron. "Thump, this is Blackout. Drop zone is clear!"

The drop ship rocketed past them, spinning to orient the doors for Gamma Team's exit. Jason shook his head as he could see Jaw-Jack holding on to the frame and Thump laughing.

"God, that woman is crazy," he mumbled. Then, on the comm to his companions, "Alright, let's get in the air and sweep the area for any stragglers."

KEITH MOVED OVER TO the door of the drop ship. He took hold of the handle and looked back at everyone. Each team member placed their left hand on the shoulder in front of them as they got in line. Once the last one did so, they tapped the shoulder twice. Keith took a deep breath as the chain reached him, telling him the go was on him. No pressure.

He squeezed the lever, slid the door open, and surged forward, bringing up his rifle. He panned left and right, then pointed the muzzle of his weapon at the airlock door. Keith made his way towards it in a quick but smooth shuffle step. The rest of the team moved so close he felt them against him. The line was like one long living organism.

He knew every rifle in the team was oriented outward, scanning for a target. Keith was positive everything in the hangar was dead. The hail of kinetic fire from the Tiger Sharks took care of that. Bodies and debris from the places they had sought cover littered the space. Still, in the off chance someone was lurking in an EV suit, they stayed wary.

As the team advanced up to the access door, Keith checked the seal. It was engaged, protecting the station from decompression. Most stations with sections exposable to hard vacuum had them. They were arrayed in combination with a central deflection wall just before each door. This allowed people to access damaged areas and repair them while in EV suits. It also gave someone a last chance in case of explosive decompression. The problem for his team was that it was only a couple feet past the door. Keith would have to put his people at risk getting in.

Keith placed a device on the door that was designed to override the safety feature in the computer. The doors functioned separately from the main power grid in case of power failure. This device could access most of the security features for emergencies if the door was closed due to an emergency decompression and not an alert. Most security systems blocked this override out for just such situations.

He hoped they had not hardened their system against this form of intrusion. If not, Plan B was to force the door open. The device did its job, however, accessing the door's emergency lock out and overriding it. He let out a held breath and gave a thumbs up to the rest of the team. The system beeped and the door slid open, a brief flush of air from within exiting into the hangar. Keith stepped in first, as he always told himself to, followed by the rest of second squad. First squad would come in behind them, led by Commander Jubert. The narrow hallway led to the next safety door. Heavy bolts clicked into place as the air stabilized.

He fired a shot from his rifle at the observation window, the high-speed armor-piercing rounds more than a match for the safety glass. The sound of the rifle was slightly muffled by the suits, but Keith felt it as well. The glass shattered, raining against the back wall and the floor offset by the metallic thud into the safety wall. He signaled the next in line, Granberg, who pulled out a small grenade. Once against the door, Keith moved to the side as Granberg pulled the pin and dropped the grenade into the hall beyond. Shouts were cut short as it detonated, vibrating the door. The sounds of fragments ricocheted off the walls, and bodies and equipment hit the floor with distinct thuds.

Keith pulled an optical cord from his forearm and pushed it through the open window, panning left and right. He smirked at Granberg, who was stepping back, then cued up his com. "Pew-Pew, pop this door."

Silverling surged from the back of the line. Keith watched as she pulled out a pair of small rectangular devices. It was like she was putting presents under a scary-looking Christmas tree. She tapped in a few places, nodded, and then planted three devices on the door, one on each hinge and one on the latch keeping it closed.

"Alright, set. Back up, chief," she said over the com, still in the enclosed EV mode of their suits.

He backed up with her until they were with the rest of the team, ten feet away. Again, hands were on shoulders. Once the chain of squeezes made it to Keith, he tapped her twice. The door blew off its points of contact with the surrounding seal, folded in half by the force. It thumped into the wall beyond, that was in place to protect people from being sucked out in decompression.

Keith moved forward, leading the team down the next corridor, around the deflection wall. His eyes darted to the bodies on the floor. Grenades did ugly work. Two, he noticed while stepping over them, had been right next to the blast when it went off. The others died from the blast wave and shrapnel, as evident from bleeding mouths and ears and multiple entry and exit wounds. As his weapon panned, he observed a blood trail. One pirate was crawling down the hall, his legs dragging along.

"Don't move!" Keith called.

The wounded man rolled over, holding up a plasma pistol. It never got leveled on a target as Keith and the commander opened fire. The man fell back limp, the pistol clattering to the floor.

After prodding him with his boot, Keith motioned everyone forward. They advanced through another set of doors to the base of the control room stairs. The space didn't allow for a lot of cover, on the steps or before them. Keith stopped just out of view, angling to see up the steps. *Not much to work with*, he thought, noting how some lights put shadows on the celling. There was movement, and he heard people moving around, likely forming a defensive circle. Keith motioned at Granberg and nodded up the steps.

Granberg pulled out two large flashbangs and moved to a space between both squads, pulled the pins and tossed both grenades up the stairwell. The force was felt even down in the corridor. Keith had to remind himself to breathe through the initial impact. The suit did a fair job taking the sting out of the devices, but that was all. The jarring rattle he felt to his core never seemed to be stopped.

Keith used that as the cue to move forward up the steps, the others on his heels. He knew Granberg was on the far side of the stairs and Silverling was bringing up the middle. Each would take a section of the next room. As Keith topped the stairs and turned, panning his weapon over his section, he saw a man and two women standing there, reeling from the blast, their hands covering their ears or trying to reach for their dropped weapons. Target response and muscle memory was all he felt as he opened fire, moving from target to target.

He pressed the attack with Silverling and Granberg, moving forward and away from the stairs. They made room for the next shooters to come up the stairs. He knew the rest of the team was pressing up to support them and follow up on their shooting. He had to be sure each threat was down, putting three rounds in each before moving on.

Keith swept the muzzle of his rifle back and forth, looking for any threats moving by the various terminals around the room. The room was set up like any typical hangar control center—a set of stations rounding the room and an oversight post with a small horseshoe-shaped station of monitors.

Apart from the dead bodies.

He looked from one to the next to see if any follow up was needed. Lifeless eyes looked back at him or off into the void. The first woman he came across had fallen against the oversight post's terminal. Keith looked quickly to the next two in his target spread, finding a man and woman in a heap together. The woman had grabbed the man as he fell. Her wounds were high on her chest and her hand was hooked under the man's arm. He shook his head as he watched the blood pool.

"Clear right!" Keith called.

Granberg answered, "Clear left!"

"Clear center!" came the third call out by Silverling.

Keith breathed a sigh—no casualties amid the shooters. He glanced back and watched the rest of the team come up. Commander Jubert, Harrison, Newsie, and another six operators were the last up the steps.

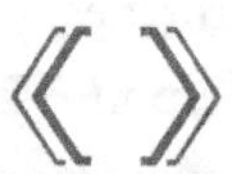

JOHN HAD HIS SUIT-MOUNTED camera running and the drone flying. He was recording all the footage he could. The more he made, the more he would have to work with when he built his story. The sight at the top of the steps, however, gave him pause. He watched as the others moved past him, except for Andrews. The man's hand was firmly on his shoulder and almost felt oppressive. John glanced at him and moved forward into the room, surprisingly, with no resistance from his escort, just the constant feel of his hand holding his shoulder.

"You going to do that the whole time?" he asked.

Andrews chuckled. "Well, it wouldn't go well for me to let you get shot. Seriously though, it's the best way to control where you go if it goes bad. So, get comfy." John rolled his eyes but relented. He focused on the rest of the team as they went about their work. Holte and Silverling were collecting weapons from the men and women on the floor. With each one they picked up, they pulled out the power pack or ejected the magazine, tossing them aside. Eversley and Granberg were moving bodies to the side of the room near the window that looked out over the hangar. Quireshi went through all their pockets, creating sorted piles of what she found.

He watched it all, silent, and yet conflicted. He couldn't really explain why he felt like asking why they didn't try to arrest them. He had been told the grenade that had been thrown up here was non-lethal, yet they used deadly force with their rifles. The attack had been fast and brutal; he had watched the footage from Keith's helmet camera. Yet, in checking the remains and setting up, the operators were professional. Not a one made a joke about the shooting skills of another or the damage to the bodies. They even arrayed them in rows.

I'm a journalist, he told himself. *I need to record this.*

The team was so quiet and meticulous going about their work, John almost jumped when Jubert spoke.

"Set up the command post here," Jubert ordered as he removed a dead pirate from the console. She fell to the floor unceremoniously, then Bekele collected her and took her to the side with the others.

John moved aside as portable computers were set up to take over the computer systems in the room, converting the hangar control deck into a working command post. Computers hacked into the security network, taking over camera feeds and internal sensors. As they did so, Qureshi brought over some of the things she had found on the dead. She and Keith read through papers and tablets, looking for something.

"What's all that about?" John asked Andrews.

Andrews looked over and then back to him. "Intel hunting. They'll read any tablet or letters those pirates had on them and determine what is useful and what isn't."

John watched it all with a sort of detached fascination. He had expected them to be piled up and generally spat upon. These people had attacked their fellow citizens and killed helpless individuals. Yet, the operators who just killed them still acted with a mix of honor and decency. He stopped and snapped a photo with the drone of Qureshi and Eversley giving last rights and praying over them.

Commander Jubert's voice reached his ears through the com. "New data coming in."

Everyone in the team glanced at their HUD as the layout of the compound came to life. John looked at it all, then back to Andrews. "How do you understand any of this?" he asked over a private comm channel.

Andrews shook his head slightly and took his hand off the shoulder to hold up a single finger. John looked at his links and saw that channel one was being used on the radios between the combat suits. He changed to listen.

"Nothing exotic. Seems like a basic prefab," Keith was saying.

Holte joined in. "Yeah, three sections overall. Those broken down into subsections. Converted mining station, most likely."

"I see the habitat section is divvied up: barracks, recreation, mess hall. Stairwell access. It looks to me like they sank a mine shaft and, once they cleared out the space, built into it. Only one access point," Keith replied.

"Looks like the industrial section is the same. Machine shop, storage, more storage. I'm willing to bet that's where they are keeping them," Holte continued.

John started to ask a question but was cut off by the commander. "This isn't all of it. This place likely has surprises left in it."

The words made him stop his line of thought. John considered what other things might be there. He decided it was best to let them sort it out. He took a deep breath and winced. The air in the suit had a terrible scent to it, and for just an instant, he wondered why. Then the fact that he was panting made sense. He'd take a breath mint with him next time.

His attention went to Keith, who was changing out his rifle's magazine. John stepped over, his escort in tow. As he watched, Keith started to reload the magazine and put it on his belt. He looked up as John got close.

"This should be an interesting shootout," Keith commented.

John looked at him. "Are you looking forward to it?"

Keith shrugged. "Only in that it's a dynamic situation. I have to be mindful of it at all times. Battle is fluid, Newsie. I have to plot the best course that gets them all home safe." John had his next question again cut off by Commander Jubert. "Alright, facial software is up, so all hostages will appear on your HUDs marked as live objectives."

John hesitated to look at the feed. He remembered the people who had been brought back to the colony. He shivered and made himself look. The faces of those missing scrolled past, listing name, occupation, living location. Everything he imagined was known about them. He prayed silently they had been spared the horrors of torture so far.

Then he heard Holte's voice. "Got 'em! Hostages are in the storage area of the machine shop. Looks like most of them."

John felt his heart leap into his throat at the callout. He spun to look, only to have it displayed on his HUD like everyone else. He felt his head spin at the shift in field of view. He stopped moving and took a moment, then looked at the hostages shown on the feed Holte was sharing.

There were maybe a dozen people huddled together, some sleeping, some awake, staring at the door or the camera. The facial recognition software cycled through them, small arrows on his HUD showing identified people.

"I bet we find a few in the barracks as entertainment," Qureshi growled.

John wanted to be sure he got all their expressions, showing that they were bothered by such barbarity. They were still human beings who had to kill their fellows. In an age when many different species interacted with Earth, humans couldn't afford to kill one another off and had to hold tight to their own humanity.

"Same rules as ever, find them and effect rescue. Cut down any opposition to that!" Jubert called out, bringing everyone back to center. "Mind on mission. You all know just as well as I do what could be the case here. These people are capable of anything, so expect the worst, hope for the best, and deal with everything in between.

"Looks like one corridor leads to a split, and then you'll go your separate ways. First squad, Holte, Eversley, Harrison, Hughes, and Bekele, you'll go secure the bulk of the hostages we've located."

A chorus of yes sirs and first squad formed up, Holte taking point, followed by Eversley as her support. The medic, Hughes, took center, followed by Harrison and Bekele bringing up the rear. Most of them were not small. However, the massive Bekele made each of them look like children.

"Second squad gets all the fun," Keith commented as he moved up near Holte. John watched with fascination as they moved, keeping as much direct footage from his helmet camera as he could. The others moved up with him, the smaller Silverling taking the second position. Stewart, the largest of the group and team medic, formed the center. Behind him came Qureshi and Granberg, who, while not small, were not the imposing physical presences Bekele was on the other team.

John eyed the axe on Granberg's belt and inadvertently shivered. The thing was clearly not just for show; he carried it into battle.

Commander Jubert looked back at his team and nodded. "Get it done. Get home." John tapped a few keys, sending his drone to follow second squad. They were going into a certain fight. He wouldn't be allowed to go with them. Once the drone was following them, he looked at Holte and the commander. "We go with first?"

Commander Jubert glanced at Andrews, who shrugged, then looked at Holte, who nodded. The commander motioned him on, and he and Andrews took position at the rear of the team. Andrews had planted him directly behind Bekele. John looked back as Andrews shot him a look.

"I'm rear guard now. I've got our six. You hit the floor if anything happens. I won't be as able to direct you."

"Six?" John asked.

"Our backs. Six o'clock...behind us?" Andrews pressed.

"You get me shot, Newsie, and I will haunt you." Holte glared.

The entire team chuckled, hands again on the shoulders in front of them. John watched as Keith and Holte looked at one another and exchanged a fist bump. He made a mental note to use that image; it would be a key part of his story. He was brought from his musing as the team moved with him, caught in its motion.

The corridor was at a slight downward angle and otherwise unremarkable, with riveted steel walls showing it was a prefabricated system. The flooring was unimpressive, covered in a slip proof black rubber. There weren't even overhead lights, only the glow from the visors of their suits.

They came to the diverging point of the corridor, a single stair well up and down at a forty-five-degree angle. There was some light here as hanging lamps had been installed. More of the same material met them here, now with steps.

"Happy hunting," Eversley said.

Keith countered, "Don't shoot the wrong people, eh?"

"Fuck too! You don't blow the place up!"

Both teams moved in opposite directions—first squad towards the hostages and the handful of pirates guarding them. Second squad moved into the wolf's den. They would be keeping all the rest of the of the enemy force pinned down. As they moved apart, John almost felt bad for the pirates. They did not know the sort of hell that was coming their way.

AS SECOND SQUAD MOVED down the hall towards the habitat section, Keith motioned a change in stance. The team shifted, Silverling at Keith's side now, Qureshi and Granberg doing the same. Stewart, a few paces back, turned, watching behind them now. Unobserved hatches were a thing in pirate bases.

Second squad approached the next corridor interchange just as a small group of pirates rushed through the door. They hadn't expected the squad to be right outside. Seeing the approaching assault team sent them into panic. Two men tried raising their rifles but froze midway. A woman tried to unholster her pistol before she released the restraining lock.

"Contact front!" Keith barked as he and Silverling knelt.

Their weapons clear of obstacles, Granberg and Qureshi opened fire at the same time as their teammates. Ballistic rounds and high energy pulses of laser fire burned the molecules in the air between them and their targets. The stench of ozone and burnt flesh filled the air as energy struck the two with the rifles. Keith and Granberg's ballistic rounds found their marks on the woman with the pistol stuck in her holster.

Keith watched the corridor for more movement before calling clear and moving the team forward. "Pew-Pew, I want a swarm grenade announcing us into the next open area."

Silverling used her left hand to grab the explosive cluster device out of her hip pouch. A quick tap of the safety and she inserted it into the launcher positioned underneath her weapon's muzzle. Despite the intensity of the coming moments, she had a grin on her face hidden by the visor.

Keith called for them to stack up as the door loomed closer. They all formed a single line again. Eyes ahead and behind.

A quick glance with the optical cord and he saw the room beyond. A hodgepodge barricade of tables, chairs, modular boxes and crates, with people moving beyond it. In the center was a massive machine gun.

Keith suspected the gun was a hundred years old, dating back to the Middle Eastern wars on Earth. A large muzzle that had to be .50 calibers in width and an ammo belt visible at about chest height. Smaller arms flanked it on either side, as well as a pair of coilguns—military grade, by the look of them, and shiny new. Through the various holes in the barricade, he saw people moving back and forth and manning the mounted guns pointed at the doorway.

"Nice set up if we planned on running into our deaths," Silverling commented as she viewed the feed on her HUD.

"Pity, we plan on killing them." Keith smirked.

Silverling grinned and took a position just outside of the line of sight and then kneeled, rifle pointed to the corner of the door. Once Keith nodded, she leaned, coming into view of the guns in the defensive line. She squeezed the trigger on her launcher.

The launcher made a sort of popping sound, like some child's toy cork gun. It was almost drowned out by the shouts from inside the room as the screaming pirates called out, "Incoming!". Silverling's grenade exploded just above the defensive line.

Swarmer grenades, like any typical grenade, filled the air with shrapnel accelerated by the blast. These small fragments tore into flesh and even body armor. To make the swarmer worse, it was filled with tiny metallic spheres with delayed micro charges. These detonated after bouncing off nearby walls or after embedding themselves in softer flesh or armor.

A chorus of explosions and screams told Keith that the secondary aspects had gone off. He pivoted and brought his rifle into the ordeal. His mind was fully under his training's grasp. Muscle response and mental distancing all met as he moved. The pirates became targets, places he had to put rounds into to move and protect his team. This all came together, and as Keith found a target still upright and trying for one of the rail guns, he squeezed the trigger.

The shots connected in a short burst of fire. He swiveled to the next target and fired again, then panned the room. Beside him, he could feel Silverling, Granberg, and Qureshi opening fire and sweeping their weapons. Return fire was sporadic as the enemy fell back to other positions outside the room, exiting through the two other exits.

"Move up and engage. I want them on their heels till we clear out!" Keith called out. A staccato of gunfire filled the air from Qureshi and Granberg as they advanced towards a doorway. A token resistance of two male pirates armed with ballistic rifles and dressed in work clothes melted as the two operators closed the distance. Keith and Silverling advanced to another door, firing at a man stepping out.

Peering through the optical camera, Keith took in the room. This one looked like the barracks sleeping space. Bunks that likely had been in orderly rows now laid on their sides in clusters, creating various hiding places for people to take cover.

Commander Jubert's voice came over the radio. "This is over-watch to second squad. Be advised, first squad has encountered stiff resistance. You will be holding longer than planned. What's your status?"

Keith keyed up his mic. "Status is green, minor enemy contact. Ten enemy KIA. No casualties on our team."

"What sort of contact are you taking?"

Keith looked around across the room. Eying the dead bodies and the equipment they had, he also accounted for the barricade they tossed up and the old machine gun that was well kept, the military grade rail guns, and the rifles.

"Mixed. These fuckers are being supported by serious money. Problem is they aren't doing much in the training aspect. Military grade hardware, but no training to speak of. Most of it looks like ours. The rifles, though, seem to be off an ET market."

"Copy that, extra-terrestrial black market. Any non-human contacts?"

"Negative. So far, all homosapiens."

"Any contact with our missing civs?"

Keith shook his head, then keyed the mic. "Negative. Though I think some are nearby. We've got a good hold point in some sort of common area. Looks like the barracks and the recreation space. We've got contacts in both areas."

With that, he closed the channel and went back to work. He glanced back over at Granberg and Qureshi. "See anything?"

Granberg shook his head and grunted. Qureshi did much the same, though both stayed crouched at the door. Optical cords pointed around the corners, panning the room. "If they're in there, they are hunkered and not moving. Probably trying to get a feel for things, or maybe slipping into hidey-holes," came Granberg's eventual reply.

Keith looked at his HUD and considered a few ideas, then settled on an easy one. He activated his combat suit's loudspeaker. "If anyone in there can hear me, speak up." He smiled when he heard the sound of shuffling and arguing.

"What do you want, soldier boy?" came a gruff voice in response.

Keith grinned. "Well, let's start with your surrender. Then we'll argue and settle on you giving me any of the people you guys have hiding in there from the convoys."

"What the fuck are you babbling about? We aren't gonna surrender to be executed! We sure as hell aren't going to give you the only things keeping you from blowing up the room." Keith shook his head. "Well, at least we made it to the second one pretty quick." He keyed the speaker back up. "You won't be executed. You'd have to be tried and convicted and then be deemed responsible enough to face—"

A burst of gunfire at his cover cut him off. "Shut yer mouth and fuck off!"

"I'll make you a counter. You give me the convoy crew. Then my team and I will withdraw. So long as we aren't pressed, we won't shoot anyone." He let the offer tread water for a moment. "The other side of it means we walk over your bodies."

"You try that, and ours won't be the only bodies on the floor. I can promise you that!"

Keith nodded. "True. You'll kill your hostages. You may get lucky and put enough rounds into one of us to score a kill. I still win. The only way you win is if I get the hostages alive."

He couldn't make out details, but the differences in tone and the occasional elevated shout said the pirates were arguing amongst themselves which, to Keith's mind, was beneficial. The more infighting that occurred, the better it was for them. Once the voice of dissension started, it was hard to silence—especially by force. The man speaking had to know the fact they were in the corner. The best outcome was to save as much face as possible.

The best chance was to keep them wanting to get out of it all alive. If he could appeal to the need to survive, then maybe—just maybe—they'd lay down arms. To be fair, it was a long shot. Most of them didn't know just what was waiting for them on the other side of the wall. He looked at Stewart. Keith remembered recruiting him from a negotiation team, so this sort of made it his thing.

"Stewart, any ideas?" he asked, though he felt he knew the answer.

Stewart shook his head. "Not much. They are convinced that they only live as long as the hostages do. They may try to make a deal to walk out."

"Not my favorite option. Least not till first squad is clear," Keith said.

Stewart shrugged. "Well, I mean, there isn't much to work with. We came in planning on going loud and keeping attention on us. These guys maybe having civs here and not with the others kind of screwed that up."

Keith nodded and looked back at his optics. They were keeping attention on them, but this bog-down meant the enemy had time to organize. If there were tunnels, they could be getting into them and be flanking any of the other positions.

It was their home turf, after all. Qureshi interrupted his thought process. "Hey! I got one of the civs!"

Her feed went to all the HUDs in the squad, a blue marker and a hit on facial recognition. Andrew Markovisk. Thirty-two years old, citizen of Tronis Utopia. Looking at the feed, Keith winced; the man had clearly been abused. His shirt was covered in dried blood. None of his bruises looked treated, and he was currently being used as a human shield.

"Well, good." Keith replied, "That's one. I bet there are a couple more."

"Hey big and loud," Keith called over the loudspeaker, "I have an idea to get this moving a bit. Send me one of your hostages. Say, Mr. Markovisk."

"So, he can tell you how many and where we are!"

"Well, partly. Though I expect you'll move around after, so not much point in that," Keith countered. "My reasoning is two-fold. Giving me one hostage gets you credit and lets me know how many hostages and how you've treated them. It also shows you're willing to work with us, and we can discuss what it will take to get the rest of them."

Someone started to argue and, to Keith's ear, it was something about what sort of plan something was. It was silenced by a loud, growling voice. They weren't united at this point. That was both good and bad. Stewart caught his attention, and he read the expression. He only shrugged. As a former negotiator, Stewart should have been the one doing the talking, but now there was no going back.

"Alright," came the voice again, though it sounded farther back in the room than before. "He's coming out."

Keith nodded, even though he knew the guy couldn't see him. "Mr. Markovisk, I want you to walk to the door, and as soon as you are through, you'll turn right and come talk to me, alright?"

Hearing a weak affirmation, he motioned to Silverling. He wanted her ready to grab the guy and pull him clear of the door so the pirates couldn't just shoot him before they got any intel. It was the man's best chance to survive and not let the pirates make a point. Qureshi made a quick motion with her hand at Granberg. He leaped over and fired through Keith and Silvering's door, dropping the approaching individual. Shouts erupted. A moment later, multiple explosions shook the room.

"Fucking hell!" Keith barked as he felt the wall shudder.

Granberg and Qureshi were already exchanging fire around their door, alternating positions to keep fire in the room. Silverling and Keith opened up from their side as well. Keith cued his mic up as the firefight erupted. "Second squad, all units! Trojan horse! I say again, Trojan horse!"

"Trojan horse confirmed!" Jubert's voice came back in a rush. Soon, so did Holte's.

"Contact six!" Stewart called out from the team's rearguard position.

Keith looked back to the rear space of the room Stewart had called from. He watched Stewart firing back around the corner to the stairs they had come down. Granberg and Qureshi were now engaged with unseen shooters in the other room. He signaled Silverling to hold her position, and he bolted over to help. When he saw into the space beyond, he swore. These pirates were equipped in full tactical gear and combat suits.

"Well, this day just keeps getting better and better."

JOHN LOOKED AT ANDREWS since the last message from second squad confused and concerned him. He knew things were bad, but he wanted to know exactly what the call had meant. The effect it had on the team concerned him as well. He looked at the faces and saw grim, almost angry expressions. Holte stepped over and motioned to the helmet. John eyed the communications icon, so it activated and tied him into the network. "Alright, Newsie, we've got an issue."

John nodded. "I suspected that with the way you shoved me off the comm line." He motioned to the others. "And their looks."

Holte shrugged, and he saw that look she had when he was getting the helmet on. "The situation has changed. Everyone is now a potential hostile. Trojan horse, the sign used when the enemy is changing the terms. In this case, they are using the civs as a weapon."

"Christ, what happened?" he asked.

Holte shrugged. "Not sure, but looks like they sent a hostage with a bomb out to Keith."

John swallowed hard, his throat suddenly dry. "So, what do we do now?"

Andrews answered. "We don't do anything. I'm taking your ass back to the command post."

John started to argue, but Holte held up her hand. "That's not gonna happen either. I can't send you two back alone. Who knows what sort of shit they have waiting in a corridor. Keith has already reported they are getting organized. We've lost the initiative. This is now a slog. You two are staying with first squad."

Andrews nodded and shot John a look that felt heated. John supposed it was due to the fact it meant more babysitting. He looked to Holte, who was offering a drone, not unlike what he had sent to watch second squad.

"You're on the drone. If we all get out of this, maybe I'll let you keep the footage."

John suspected it had more to do with giving him something to do than anything else. An idle hand was a detriment; that much he had learned. With him on the drone, they all could focus on being in the fight, so he nodded.

John was shoved down, Andrews' hand firmly in place on his shoulder as he bounced off the frame of a workstation. Various weapons went off:the crack of the ballistic guns, the high-pitched fwip of the lasers, and telltale whooshing sound of plasma. A coilgun firing rattled his bones.

Every time he tried to move, Andrews' hand forced him closer to the floor. He was going to get pushed through it at this rate. The station floor shook as rounds from one weapon or another hit. His heart pounded in his ears. He felt the pressure release from his shoulder, only to have it replaced with the full weight of a person.

John looked up as best he could. Andrews was fighting with someone. He wanted to help but wasn't sure where Andrews ended, and this attacker started. The answer came quick as the combatants rolled off him. He took in a deep breath and saw the attacker reaching for a pistol.

John lunged and got his hands on it just as the attacker did. They struggled for a moment. John saw a flash out of the corner of his eye. He looked and regretted it as Andrews drove a knife into the face of the attacker. His stomach tightened and churned as Andrews pulled back the knife and the pirate's hand went limp, the body jerking.

Andrews stood and fired his gun. John's eyes were locked on the person he just watched die in front of him. "You've seen dead bodies before, John," he told himself in a quivering voice.

He reminded himself that while he had indeed, he had yet to see a life ended directly, to be face-to-face with the person as things simply stopped. He felt his stomach flop again, and an acidic bile burned its way up his throat. The visor of his suit opened, allowing him to puke on the floor. Nothing came out though, just the burn of acid in his throat.

An eerie calm settled over the area. None of the soldiers called to each other. They just sat, silent and waiting. Risking it, John moved his head up and looked around the room. Holte and Eversley eyed the corridor Bekele had fired down. He was on the left, and they were on the right. Harrison and Andrews watched the hallway they had come down before this space. He looked at Holte; she was motioning to her helmet.

John tapped the side of his helmet and the communication options appeared on his HUD. He looked for the one marked for the squad. There were a few beeps and then a click as the encryption systems linked up. Soon enough, he heard her voice over the headset.

"Newsie, you up yet?"

He nodded and gave her a thumbs up. He still didn't trust his voice to be stable. Though he knew better, he hoped none of them would take note. In all truth, they wouldn't care, but he still had some ego. Toughness was still a thing.

"Well, looks like you are up enough."

Her tone was somewhere akin to the same as the joke about him asking Silverling for drinks. It was likely she was smiling despite the firefight. He gave her his best annoyed look. "I'm fine."

"Hey, he managed not to puke. Good. Send your camera down the hall and check the room beyond."

He blinked, and then noticed the drone control on the HUD. He gave the guidance a few way points then activated it. He gave Holte a thumbs up just as the feed came on. Watching the feed, he wasn't sure about the vomit issue. Grenades had made a considerable mess of the pirates in the next area—limbs were torn off and the bodies perforated by shrapnel. He saw the larger space did little to offer protection from the swarmers and fragmentation grenades.

John saw various tables and stacks of crates setup to offer cover for a fight only to be no match for Gamma's assault; they all laid in random states of destruction. The tables were shattered, the crates having large holes in them. Some of the metal was scorched by flame from the blast.

"Fuck."

He wasn't sure who said it, but he echoed the sentiment. As he was about to close it out, a door slid open on the far side of the room. He spun the camera to see a woman in fatigues with a belt, no armor, and very pregnant stepping out. She was holding a plasma rifle, but not up and ready. More drooping and resigned. As she stepped out, she dropped it to the floor with a clatter and spoke. "They're all dead now," she called out in a horse unsteady voice.

Holte switched on the PA on her suit and spoke in a calm, soothing tone. "This is Petty Officer First Class Sasha Holte of the United Nations Space Corps. What's your name, miss?"

John blinked and looked over towards the squad leader. He seldom heard that sort of care in her tone. She would find it soothing, except for the nasty amounts of gore in the room. Well, he had to admit that was unfair. She was often that way with other members of the team.

"Leanna," the woman answered, her voice soft and distant.

"Okay, Leanna, who are you talking about? The hostages?"

"There never were any."

"What?"

Leanna's voice came back as a shriek. "It was a trap! They set this up so we could show we were ready!"

The other operators looked at each other. John felt his own heart rate jump. Every nook and cranny of the space station was now suspect. How many other awful surprises were in place? And who were 'they'?

John stood up more and looked around. He adjusted the camera on the drone so that it was watching Leanna as she spoke, zooming in so she was the dominate part of the picture. Though he thought he should be looking at the rest of the room, the journalist in him wanted the image of the woman confessing the horrible truth of the situation.

Holte got on the comms as quick as she could. "One-one to Overwatch. We have a problem."

The commander's voice came back. "What sort of problem?"

Holte relayed the recent development. The room full of dead pirates and the sudden appearance of the woman named

Leanna. Even her announcement. That seemed the most troublesome news. If the people they came to save weren't here, then what were they supposed to do? Who had they seen? John's head spun.

The silence on the other end of the line was frustrating. John paced, looking at the room and the bodies from the fighting. He kneeled and looked at a patch on one of the uniforms. He didn't recognize it at all, so he tapped Andrews' leg. "What's this?"

Andrews' voice was tense. "What, Newsie?"

John ignored it. "This patch. Is this military?"

Andrews leaned against him and studied the patch in question. "Holy shit. Holte!"

John wondered if the expression on her face was the last thing people saw when a large predator rushed them, cold, angry, and compassionless. She moved away from Eversley and came over. John had to fight the urge to shrink. He knew she wasn't going to hurt him, but her sheer presence at that moment was intimidating.

"Gods." Her voice was flat, almost a mix of annoyance and anger.

John felt it was safe to press his question. "What is it?" he asked again, amazed his voice was so steady.

"That's a Shezlan special forces patch," she answered.

John blinked. "Shezlan, as in the Prides of Thyla? Those Shezlan?"

"Yes, Newsie, the ones that tried to bomb Earth forty-some years ago," Andrews snapped.

Holte shot him a look and then turned to John. "Newsie, I know you are already sort of doing it, but I need documentation of all the stuff here. Not like a journalist, but evidence collection. Alright?"

John nodded and set his helmet's camera to snap photos. He and Andrews moved amid the bodies. As Andrews pulled out paperwork, John photographed it. They worked their way around the room as Holte added to her report. This time John smiled; she hadn't shoved him out of the comm channel.

As usual, the commander's voice was cold, absent of emotion. The constant professional, he knew what to tell them and where to look.

"We ran the facial recognition software over the girl. She was one of the people on the transport, and if what she is saying is true, then we have a very serious problem. We need intel."

Holte nodded, though she knew he couldn't see it. "Copy. We are gathering what we can from the bodies here. Secure her and get out of here?"

"Sweep the next area and double check. The machine room should be just on the left side of that area. Might be that they are just keeping the ones who didn't want to play along there. Once done, bring that woman and anyone else back here. Second is getting pressed hard. Clock's ticking."

Motions set them to work as now more attention went to watching the rear for an ambush. John watched and then changed his camera back to record. He felt comfortable in his job and elected to stay in that mindset. Documenting the team doing their work, John looked back at the hall at the same time Holte and Eversley did. All eyes went to Leanna, who was standing there crying.

"Leanna? It's Sasha. I need you to do something for me. I need you to raise your hands and step towards my voice."

Leanna nodded and walked forward. She was looking their way, but her expression was distant. It was like she was not seeing any of the area she was in. She sniffled and whimpered as she walked, and when Holte told her to stop where she was, her eyes widened in fear.

"You need to take a deep breath and relax, Leanna. I'm not going to hurt you. Neither is my friend. We need to be careful, though. I want you to lift your shirt about halfway up and turn around in a circle."

Eversley watched down the scope of his rifle. The poor girl's hands were a blur. The sniffling and whimpering continued as she raised her shirt and turned as Eversley watched for any weapons or explosives. She finished her circle, then glanced at Holte. He shook his head. He saw nothing of risk.

"Alright, Leanna, I know it's gonna be hard, but I need you to put your hands on top of your head and walk backwards down this hall."

Her voice shook as she replied, "What if I fall? It's... It's..."

"I know. Just look up and walk backwards. My friend will move and put his hand on your back, okay?"

Leanna looked at the corridor and retched. She cried again and repeated she was sorry and became unsteady on her feet. Still, she managed to do as told, shuffling backwards as she looked at the ceiling.

John watched through the drone camera. When he tried to look around the corner, Eversley leaned against his leg and told him to back up. John glanced down, but Eversley was looking down his rifle. Still, he explained, "Dude, I know you're just looking to know. If there is an ambush, it'll happen when we are in the hall. Just wait till I get her back far enough to be out of any firing line."

John nodded. He had no desire to get shot. Just as he was about to speak, Eversley moved up the hall towards Leanna and grabbed the center of her shirt. "Okay, I have you. We're gonna walk quick."

Once she was hustled out of the hallway, he moved to the side and had her face the wall. John didn't step close, but he moved to see what was happening. After a thorough but gentle search for weapons, Eversley nodded to Holte, giving a thumbs up and stepped back. John was sure he heard Eversley let out the breath he'd been holding the whole time. Holte moved over and spoke, "Leanna. Take a deep breath. Now I need to know what you meant by no hostages."

She didn't answer at first. John kept his camera back behind Holte but zoomed in so he could document the scene. The woman's face was streaked with still-falling tears, the red in her eyes leaving almost no white at this point. "There never were any. Everyone on the ship with me was brought here to train and fight. Anyone who didn't join them, they...they used as targets."

"If that is the case, why are you surrendering?" Holte kept her voice gentle as she prodded the woman.

"I'm pregnant," she answered. "I came with my boyfriend. After it started, I couldn't do it anymore. I wasn't in the training, but I watched. I watched what they were turning us all into."

"Who's they?"

Leanna turned and looked at her with a tormented expression. Shaking her head against the wall, she stayed silent.

"Okay, you are coming with us," Holte said.

Leanna started crying again, but she did not resist. John watched Eversley tie her hands with quick strips, the clicking sound the only noise in the room.

"Alright, Andrews, Bekele, Hughes, Harrison, you four are on rearguard now. Make sure no one sneaks up on us. Eversley, you, Newsie, and I will go check the objective room. We get lucky, and we can get some of these people out of here,'" Holte said.

John blinked, but before he could ask or protest, Holte and Eversley ducked into the hall Leanna had just come from. He scrambled to keep up, setting his drone to follow him. The room beyond the hall looked just as bad in person as it did via drone. He stopped cold.

His eyes went to the bodies on the floor. He was no longer distanced by the camera feed; here they were in full color and viscera. He had to put his hand on the wall as his head spun from the copper smell. Searching for something to focus on, he found Holte and Eversley's boot prints through the mess. It didn't help.

"Hey! Newsie, eyes up here, man." Holte's voice came in like the crack of the rifles. John looked up and gasped a few times, getting his breathing under control. He looked at her and nodded, moving forward to her as steadily as he could. He was concerned about slipping. How did Leanna get through so easily?

He managed to get the rest of the way out of the hall and looked back and forth. Holte and Eversley were moving towards a heavy side door. He used his drone controls to angle it towards the door. Holte gave him a thumbs up and, for some reason, he felt better.

"There's an air handler, Newsie. Send it through that," Holte said quietly.

John sent the drone up to the air handler access. The vent wasn't overly large, but the drone was small enough to move easily past the bars. With the camera, he saw the vent extending into darkness. He moved it forward and, after a few feet, noticed a second vent going into the sealed room.

"Holte! I see them. The computer has positive ID on fifteen people!" he said, then winced at how loud he spoke. He mouthed a 'Sorry,' in the direction of two angry faces.

Holte motioned him to the side of the room as she and Eversley moved to the door. John moved the drone into position to see the room better. He kept looking at the people lying on the ground or leaning against the wall. They looked as bad as the others, abused and scared. He couldn't focus on that now, so he streamed the video to Holte's and Eversley's helmets, knowing they had to watch for another Trojan horse.

"I can't see any of the pirates," he said quietly.

Holte looked back at him and nodded. "Alright. Newsie, give me a line to the drone's speaker."

John nodded and set it up. "You're on the air."

"Attention everyone. This is Petty Officer Holte of the UNSC, Gamma Squadron. We are here to rescue those who have been taken against their will. Everyone in this room is to get on the floor face down and cover their heads with their hands. Anyone who doesn't will be considered a threat. Comply, and we will start moving you out of here."

John held his breath. The people were looking around at one another and at the door. Some jumped up to run to the door, only to be yanked down by another person. Soon, everyone was lying down. He panned the camera back and forth and then looked to Holte.

She was already moving with Eversley, and some device he had seen earlier on the door. He was unsurprised when the door slid open with Holte and Eversley slipped in. Still holding his breath, he listened to the voices, his heart pounding in his ears. This was how he felt during his first firefight. Why was he so scared now?

Holte's voice broke his mental battle, even bringing his heart rate back to normal in a flash, the journalist mindset coming forward to document the chaos. So, that's what he did.

"No one move," Holte said as she entered the room. John saw her pan her weapon back and forth over the people. Eversley stayed at the entrance, doing the same with his weapon.

"Listen carefully. I am going to search you one at a time, and then you will go out the door and stand in front of my teammate out there with the camera," Holte said.

John blinked. What did she say? He looked around at Eversley, who gave him a thumbs up. The feeling of cold exhilaration filled his core

"He will be running your faces through the identification system. Once you are verified, you will sit along the wall until we get everyone out."

John searched for a wall in the room that wasn't perforated by bullets or lasers. He saw Andrews step into the room and nod at him. "Got your six, man."

John didn't have time to revel in the feeling as the first hostage came out. She was beaten and terrified. Her hair was matted to the side of her face with dried blood from either herself or one of her friends. He blinked, then heard Eversley in his comm.

"Newsie, darken your visor. Put the camera on them and run the program. Ask them the basics. Name, ID number, and where they lived. Compare it and move them to the wall." John gave the man a thumbs up and did as directed. The program ran, picking out her features and bringing up her file.

He kept her ID number on the screen, knowing he'd never remember all those numbers and letters.

"What's your name, ma'am?" John asked in his best impression of the calm voice he saw the others use so often.

"Elizabeth, Elizabeth Russell," she said shakily.

John nodded. "Where do you live?"

"Two twenty, Orbital Lane."

"Alright, go sit down at the corner of the two walls," John said as he pointed.

Elizabeth did as he said. The next person came out. He again asked the questions to verify their ID. He did so over and over as each person came out. It felt like an eternity to John, but finally, the last one sat down.

Holte's heavy hand thumped John on his shoulder. "Good work, Newsie. Let's get the hell outta here, eh?"

He nodded. He was tired. The constant up and down wore him out. There was more to do, though, and they still had to get out. He moved the drone, scanning the people's faces and getting shots of the team organizing the escape. If he focused on his work, he could ignore the soreness of his body.

Holte looked at everyone else in the squad. "Alright, saddle up. We roll out of here and kill anyone between us and the commander. Got me?"

Everyone nodded, and the process to move out of the room started. Leanna was placed in a cord restraint behind Eversley and in front of Holte. The hostages were given directions. Once everyone was ready, Eversley lead them out, moving back to the command post at double quick march. Rifles were up, aimed at every potential area an enemy could come from.

Holte got on the radio. "First squad to all elements, Romeo. I say again, Romeo."

SILVERLING AND KEITH finished their battle with the pirates in the barracks room. A quick pan showed no further resistance. They were all dead or had slipped out. They were now on the fire line with Granberg and Qureshi, exchanging fire with the pirates in tactical gear. These at least seemed to have had some training, Keith thought. He was using one of the military grade coilguns that had survived the swarmer blast earlier.

He stopped firing long enough to respond to the radio call. "Romeo confirmed."

He looked at the line and nodded. Silverling and Granberg each chambered another swarmer. Once they were ready, Keith opened up another burst of fire from the coilgun. As soon as an opening appeared, they each sent a swarmer into the far room. On the tail of the secondary blasts, Keith barked, "Let's clear out!"

Second squad laid down fire as each member moved from their position to the stairwell. Keith abandoned the coilgun and moved last. He was running low on ammo for his primary rifle, but he couldn't fall back with the massive weapon. As he got into position, he kept his rifle leveled at the corner leading from the room they just blew apart. One man in tactical gear stumbled out, blood covering his right side as he grasped at his wounds. A quick double tap from Keith's rifle stopped the man's movement.

Once second squad got back to the corridor, Keith stopped, braced at the corner, and watched the stairwell for any pursuit.

At first, none came. He heard the shuffle of boots and arguing. The pirates were decently trained but not disciplined enough to be silent.

"We are about to have contact on our six." Keith spoke into the mic of his helmet.

Granberg and Silverling were both pressed against him now. Silverling kneeled and leaned around the corner, Granberg lying on the floor. All three used the corner as cover. Qureshi and Stewart watched down the other stairwell, making sure no one was following first squad out.

Keith heard the pirates stop and narrowed his eyes. In an instant, they would round the corner, and his team would be in yet another engagement in this tight space. Ammo was a serious issue now. He ticked off the number of explosives used and how many mag changes he had observed. The math wasn't encouraging. They would be out of ammo after two minutes of sustained fire.

"They rush us, and we're gonna be in serious trouble."

Silverling and Granberg both nodded.

"We know," Silverling said.

Granberg just growled.

Keith shook his head and smiled. If it were to be this tight a situation, he couldn't hope for better people. He let out a breath and relaxed. He wanted the muscles in his hands to be loose for trigger control. Each shot needed to count.

"Overwatch to second squad. Status?"

Keith keyed his mic up. "We are holding at the separation point. Possible contact moving behind us. Waiting for contact."

"Good, copy. First squad just moved through the command post. Can you fall back to here before you take contact?"

Keith didn't like the idea of being on the run in such tight halls. However, he wanted a drawn-out fire fight even less. A quick look at the other four in the squad and he nodded. "We are going to try."

"Good. See you soon."

A few moments of thought and Keith had a course of action drawn out. He switched to his squad's comm line. "Fall back pattern six. Just like on that solar array last year."

An extra gun would be great. Reloads would be amazing. He had neither. To make it work, they would have to fall back one at a time in a staggered chain up the corridor.

Quireshi and Stewart went the farthest down the hall, about forty feet from the door. Granberg and Silverling moved away from Keith, leaving him waiting at the door to watch. He was about to move and go past both teams to start the movements again when the shooting started.

Plasma bolts lit the hallway in eerie greens and yellows. The telltale thwip sound and crackle of energy filled the air. They burst against the side of the door frame in an intense shower of sparks, and Keith momentarily lost the ability to see. He closed his eyes and turned his head as even his HUD couldn't screen out the flash. The clacking sounds of gunfire joined as well. It was time to go.

Keith let loose a burst of fire into the advancing force and then ran from the door towards his team. "Pulling back!"

Almost immediately Silverling and Granberg opened fire, their rounds going on either side of Keith to the door as he ran past them. He kept going past Stewart and Qureshi another fifteen feet, then stopped and turned, aiming the way he had just came. He watched Silverling jump to her feet, with a quick tap on Granberg's shoulder before making a mad dash of her own past Stewart and Qureshi.

Silverling passed Keith, and he held his breath while she called for Granberg. He knew the man would wait the longest to fall back. To his relief, Granberg called out, "Last one!" as he jumped and ran to his next position. Stewart and Qureshi opened fire now as Granberg passed between them. Their laser rifles not making near the noise, but certainly causing more flashes of light than the previous conventional rifle fire. The strobe-like effect was meant to be disorienting, which was an advantage for those trained to ignore it.

The plasma and rifle rounds from the pirates added their own flashes of light. The muzzle flashes and bolts of plasma answered angrily. Keith was glad the pirates were using plasma; it was more dangerous to be sure, but less accurate at range. His squad's lasers had better accuracy and range.

The violent game of leapfrog continued, each group blitzing past the next, covering each other's escape. A single constant stream of death poured back at the pirates. They were not pushing nearly as hard against the team, and Keith was grateful for that...until the bolt on his rifle locked open. He had just fired his last round.

"Pull back!"

Silverling and Granberg covered as he ran past. Once past the second group, he turned and reached for a new magazine. There was none to be had. He looked up at the advancing pirates as Qureshi and Stewart pulled back. The pirates were growing bolder now, upping the pressure on the team's retreat.

"I'm dry!"

Keith knew that the team would adjust their fall back now. He would no longer be actively suppressing the enemy. He pulled his sidearm and stayed in the middle of the formation, occasionally letting loose a few shots when he had an opening. The pistol sounded pitiful compared to the rifles in the mix.

As Granberg and Silverling moved past, he noticed Qureshi and Stewart's laser fire was showing signs of low energy. As the power packs in their rifles got lower, they automatically went to energy conservation. The output was minimal, and while less deadly, it could keep its accuracy and extended the ability to stay in a fight. For a time, at least.

They still had a hundred yards to go down the corridor. The next change out brought more bad news as he heard one of the rifles cease fire on Granberg and Silverling's turn. Silverling gave the call that she was empty a moment later.

He fired his pistol as she moved past him, watching Granberg. "Time to go!"

Granberg growled as he moved back. He was getting low on ammo as well, and probably wanted to draw fire while the rest of the squad fell back. Keith couldn't argue the sense of it, but he had no intention of leaving anyone to that fate.

"What's left?" he called to both as they regrouped behind Stewart and Qureshi.

Silverling and Granberg were doing a check. Keith hoped his mental math was wrong, that each had at least another magazine tucked away. He had no desire to try this with just handguns.

"I've got one swarmer left," Granberg called. "And half a mag."

Silverling shook her head. "Nothing."

"Fuck. Give Silverling the swarmer. We are gonna have to break and run."

While they reloaded and exchanged, Keith moved up to Stewart and Qureshi. He filled them in and then bolted back to the other two, taking position right above Silverling as she knelt and chambered the swarmer.

"Moving!"

Keith felt his heart rate increase, and he snapped off shots with his sidearm. Granberg was being conservative with his shots, giving them the most amount of time to run. Keith's hand was on Silverling's shoulder, and to his surprise, she was breathing steadily. The idea made him smile.

Things started happening in slow motion for Keith. Granberg's rifle locked open, the last round sent down range. The single ping of the casing bouncing on the floor seemed deafening. His throat went dry as he tapped Silverling to send the swarmer. Keith kept firing as they both moved to run, counting his shots. The blast from Silverling's swarmer was his cue to run.

The blast shook him from his strange state. He turned and ran, making ten steps before the secondary explosions went off. Now, it was a race. He prayed the grenade would buy his team the time needed. The mad rush his team made would have made any track and field coach proud. It wasn't enough though; the pirates regrouped and pressed their attack again. Stewart and Qureshi set up to cover for them. He almost told them to go ahead when Jubert called over the com.

"Hit the deck!"

As one, the team dropped. A torrent of fire came from the doorway. Commander Jubert stepped into view and hefted up a shoulder-fired rocket and sent the missile down the hall. Keith watched it tear down the space and detonate. The tight confines stretched the shockwave and blast uncomfortably close, but the suit took most of the heat.

The corridor was unable to withstand the force, already weakened from the detonation of the swarmer. At the site of the blast, just amid the pirates, the tunnel collapsed under its own weight and that of the stone it had been sunk in. The remaining section above Keith groaned.

Keith tapped the shoulders of Silverling and Granberg for them to each to get up and pull back. Collapsing metal behind them creaked with an ominous sound. The section above them and to the exit held for now, but Keith had no desire to test how long it was going to hold up. The floors rumbled, signaling the impacts of kinetic rounds from the Australia in orbit of the station.

"Let's get the hell out of here!" Jubert called.

JOHN WAITED WHILE FIRST squad moved the hostages from the command post to the lander. He watched and counted as second squad poured through the doorway. He very nearly let out a cheer as the last one, Keith, came through the door. He expected much the same reaction from the other members of the team, but there were only fist bumps and the handing over of ammunition. *That is just their way*, he thought, panning his camera and recovering his drone from second squad. There was still a sense of urgency in the group. The room shook and John looked at Commander Jubert.

"Why are they shooting this place up already? Aren't they supposed to wait till we get out?"

Commander Jubert pointed to the stairs leading out of the command post. "Close support fire. We needed a way to put these bastards on their heels."

John felt himself scooped up in the movement as the operators made their way out. What struck him was that they still moved with caution, checking each area before moving to the next. As they entered the hangar bay, he saw first squad waiting in a defensive circle at the back of the landing craft they had come in on. He didn't see the Tiger Sharks anywhere.

John assumed it was because the Australia was firing on the base. The Tiger Sharks would need to be out of the way. His helmet was sealed fully again, the hangar being exposed to open space. He heard the radio calls as first squad advised Thump and Jaw Jack they were about to come aboard.

He heard the call to get on the floor. He dove flat, as ordered, then heard gun fire through the suit's headset. He looked up, getting his drone and helmet camera to see.

A group of pirates had come out of a side area, firing on the team with reckless abandon. John looked back and forth, seeing both first and second squad forming into groups, moving forward to engage the threat.

He had a thought and flipped through his drone controls, finding the one that Holte had given him. "Drone up!" he called over the comms.

John moved the drone to the height of the hangar and used the camera to see the enemy. He found the target identification system and marked where the pirates were taking cover. There were a lot of pirates, maybe twenty-five attacking them.

"Good work, Newsie!"

John wasn't sure who said it, but he gave a thumbs up to the air and looked over the drone's functions. His pulse pounded but there was something else as well. He felt aware.

Fear wasn't drowning out the sounds of the fight. It wasn't crippling him as his stomach tightened into a knot. He simply had to breathe, fly the drone, mark the targets, and give the team the best chance to win the battle. He was taking it all in and worried for a moment he might get swept up and lose himself.

He found an option on the drone: weapons. John blinked. He had forgotten that his drone was stripped down, but the one Holte gave him earlier wasn't. There wasn't much—it was only so large, after all. It did, however, have an option to deploy micro charges.

"Holte, Keith that coilgun needs to go. Now!" Commander Jubert said over the comm.

"Copy that," Holte replied. "I don't have a path from where I am!"

Keith came on next. "I've got an approach. Silverling and Granberg and I can move past that large crate."

"That's a meat grinder, buddy."

John looked all over his screen and saw it. The large gun was easily as big as he was and mounted behind several hard cargo crates. The pirates only let the barrel show as it sent a hail of rounds at the team.

"Hey, I have an idea," he called out.

He had three micro charges. He moved the drone, taking it out of position, so he could have a clear shot at the coilgun. He wasn't aware the feed was being shared until he heard Commander Jubert call over the suit's comm.

"You're out of position. Move the drone back behind the barricade. Attack from behind." John blinked but nodded and did as directed, using his eyes to move the marker to the position. Once there, he noticed that the target indicator changed from red to green. He held his breath a moment and then toggled the attack button.

The gun exploded, heaving debris, parts, and the gun team into the air. He blinked at the enormity of it and looked up from his cover to see for himself.

"Holy shit." he breathed out at last.

"Hell, yeah! Get some, Newsie!"

John looked around as the verbal pat on the back came in. John didn't know how to feel right then. But he had a job to do and took the drone back to a position to track the last of the pirates. He watched the battle from the distance of the drone as the pirates fled or were killed. It felt like an eternity, but his experience thus far had told him it wasn't. Firefights seemed to feel long and drawn out, but in the end, they only lasted a few minutes.

"All clear!" came a call.

Jubert patted him on the shoulder. "Good work. Let's get out of here."

As he passed the team members, they gave him a thumbs up or a pat on the shoulder with a free hand. Their weapons were still panning, looking for another attack, but they took time to cheer him. Once on the lander, people they had saved looked at him. Fear was still in their eyes but also gratitude. As he moved by, everyone reached up to touch his hand or arm and said thank you.

He made it to a seat and sat, then recovered his drones. John held out both hands as they each swooped in from the back of the lander and settled into his palms. He downloaded his videos and put his first drone back into the air. Recording how the civilians reacted to their rescuers—the same reception he had been given, the touching and saying, 'Thank you.'

He watched the operators nod and some of them patted the people on their shoulders as they moved past. He moved the camera and recorded Keith and Holte, the last two getting on the lander. Holte first, turning and aiming her rifle out as Keith came in, saying. "Last one." The door closed, and they removed their helmets as the ship took off.

They look worn out, he thought. Sweat on their faces matted down hair. They felt the same thing he had—the wearing down of the body from repeatedly exerting themselves. They gave each other a fist bump and turned to see the people they had saved staring at them.

John wasn't sure what he expected, maybe for them to hug and laugh. Maybe to bask in the reception they received. Instead, they each just leaned against the back of the lander bulkhead and looked past everyone else. The rest of the team did the same.

Helmets off, vacant, tired expressions, and matted hair. Well, except for Granberg, whose bald head glistened as he slept, leaning his head back against the bulkhead.

John forced himself up, moving towards the front of the lander to the pilot's section. He wasn't surprised to see them both hard at work. There was no need to bother them; he looked out the window as they left the asteroid and the base.

"Hey, good to see you made it," came Jaw-Jack's comment.

John nodded. "Yep. What happens now?"

"To the base?"

John nodded again. "Yes, the base. Are they going to arrest them all now? I know there are more pirates there. They weren't all killed."

Jaw-Jack looked at him, then motioned out the window. "You'll see here in a second."

John watched as streaks of silvery mist shot across the void of space. The Australia was now firing on the base. Since Gamma had left, it was now fair game. The Australia wasted no time in unleashing all its coilguns, the impacts sending huge sprays of rock and material up into the void. The barrage lasted the entire trip back to the Australia. Once it was finished, the large rock was now several smaller ones.

He settled into the jump seat and suddenly felt very tired. He had no idea how they did it; the constant up and down of the mission was taxing. The lids of his eyes worked their way down. The conversation between the pilots drifted to muddled, distant sounds. John jerked awake. The shadow of the Australia loomed over the cockpit. Thump and Jaw-Jack were talking to the deck officers over the radio, preparing to land. Jaw-Jack looked back at him and tapped his seatbelt, then pointed to Thump. He got the hint and fastened the belts.

As the hangar came into view and they entered the field around the ship, John crossed his fingers. He felt the surge in his stomach as the ship lowered to the deck. He tensed, waiting for the impact of the landing.

"Ye of little faith," Thump called over her shoulder as she slowed the ship, the lander coming to a gentle rest on the deck. She looked back over at John, glaring at his seatbelts.

"Um. Well." John shrugged.

"Yeah, yeah. Get off my bird."

He didn't need to be told twice. He extracted himself from the belts and moved back to the main area with the team and the civilians. He was reasonably sure he was safer there than the cockpit. Confirmation came in the sounds of a thump and Jaw-Jack's yelp of pain.

As the others were escorted off, he passed Holte and handed her his recordings. That was a part of the deal he wouldn't be able to alter. He stopped as Leanna was escorted past the two of them. She was hanging her head and crying again. It stung John more than he liked to admit. The look on Holte's face was less concern and more study. He'd seen it before, in the mirror when he was working a story.

"What will happen to her?" he asked Holte.

She shrugged. "Well, likely she'll be questioned at length. Then, if all the answers are considered full enough, she'll be turned over to the Colonial Court on Tronis."

"They'll do what then? This whole ordeal has almost crippled their economy." The look on Holte's face chilled him. She knew full well what the results would be. John stared back at her and worked to breathe. "Do you care?"

"That's not in me in this case," she said, meeting his gaze. "She was a militant. If she hadn't made that call to betray them, she'd have been between us and the hostages."

John had to consider that, knowing the situation might have been different. "She didn't though. She chose, and I think she needs to be given credit for that."

"And maybe she will. For me though, she's the enemy. Granted, she stood down, but that isn't a pass. These are the calls we all make that keep us awake at night."

John shook his head, watching the scared girl get escorted through a door. He looked back to Holte and saw her looking at him this time, her expression softer, like the one she had when he was trying to seal his helmet that morning.

"What?" he asked.

Holte smiled at him. "You have that look. In over your head. Scared and wanting to know all the answers at once."

"Thanks?"

Holte laugh and patted him on the shoulder. "It's a good thing. You still get to feel like a normal person. That's something we really don't get to do. All these sorts of days are a mixed bag. We won, but we took a lot of lives. Bad people. That should be enough, but it seldom is. A life is still a life. We become hardened and appear detached and cold to outsiders."

John nodded and looked at the floor a moment. He had basically accused her of that just a moment ago. He let out a long breath and nodded. "I get it."

"Not yet, but I think you will. The hostages are safe. Focus on that, especially when you think about the rest."

He nodded and excused himself. He needed some time to think as he went to his room to get a chance to make a call. The chance came eventually as his tablet beeped, letting him know his call was waiting. Connection time was a pain, but he got on with his editor on Earth, recounting his story and what had occurred. To say the man on the other end was shocked would be an understatement.

"Jesus, John. This is ... terrifying and incredible all at once. Do you realize the sheer power of what you recorded and witnessed? You'll be the point man on the exclusive!"

"I know. It seems more complicated than that, though. These pirates had help. The weapons we found were military grade, and not all were human made. So, I think we have a lead on a serious case of non-human involvement in our affairs."

The two talked for the whole of the allotted time, discussing the possibilities of the story and the areas to start asking questions, even building their own theory as to what was going on. So many questions to answer and sort so they could take the story to the people.

The last argument hung with him, though, to go back to Earth and take the lead on the sstory. He had to admit, the editors were right: It would be a career-making story. A tell-all about pirates being supplied arms by non-humans. People being recruited from the colonies under the guise of freedom fighting. Alien governments covertly manipulating the affairs of humanity. Once it got into the air, every network would try to carry the story. People would look for answers. Being there in the main chair, breaking the story himself, he'd be the face of it.

The pragmatic side of him also knew that this team would be the lead in this ordeal. They'd be sent most often to resolve matters related to these militants. He'd learn more here and have an active hand in the investigation. The footage and insight alone would be worth more. He also had to admit they were good people. Those sorts of people tended to be forgotten in the stories, become nameless faces representing excessive force or oppression as they tried to protect people from those who would do them harm. He was in a position that would let him tell their story as well.

John slept the rest of the way to the colony, the hum of the ship knocking him out quickly. He was too exhausted for dreams, just the peaceful rest of hard work. John hadn't even bothered to undress. He'd have a few hours even after they docked before he'd get off and plenty of time to shower and get to the base.

As he left his quarters, he nearly plowed into Commander Jubert. "Commander, sorry. I didn't mean to just go barging out into anyone."

Commander Jubert waved it off. "Not a factor. I was coming by to give you this." He offered over the data drive that held his footage and commentary from the mission. He also handed over a tablet with a schedule of transports leaving for Earth.

"Okay, I know what this is." He held up the drive. "But this?"

"I figured you would want to get home as quick as possible."

"I'd like to stay actually." John was surprised at the words, but proud as well. He offered the tablet back.

Commander Jubert looked surprised. Still, he tucked the tablet into a pocket on his BDUs and nodded. With a motion down the hall, he walked along towards the elevator that led down to the decks connected to the docks.

"The idea that you want to keep getting shot at is surprising," he explained.

John nodded and laughed. "I got a similar comment from Holte this morning before we landed on the asteroid. And after we got back. We were talking about Leanna."

"I see. So, she made a point you took to heart?"

He shrugged. "I think she did. Though, I am still not sold on all of it. She has a point of view I'm having a time wrapping my head around, even if I want to think I've got it. I respect it, but I don't think I'm done learning about or telling Gamma's story."

The older man laughed, holding the door open as they took the lift. "I am sure you'll learn it. They are all at the bar at the docks. DJ's I think it's called."

"You going down?"

The commander shook his head. "No. I let them play without my oversight. You want to stay welcome, make sure you buy some beer and bring money to lose."

The trip from the Australia to the public quarter of the colony was surprisingly short. The tram system made only one stop to pick up some dock workers and then was to his stop.

The place felt peaceful, making him smile, like the shadow of threat being pulled away by turning on a lamp.

He made his way directly to the bar, still playing the same sort of music, though people seemed to be enjoying themselves a bit more. The news was broadcasting the rescue and telling who was responsible. He moved to the counter and nodded to the brown-haired woman behind it. "I'm back. Let's try this again, shall we? Can I get three pitchers of whatever they are drinking?" he asked and pointed to the back.

She smiled and sat the pitchers on the counter. "Get it to them before it gets hot. On the house."

John smiled and made his way over to the group, receiving a nod and wave from Holte and Keith, both of whom sat him across from Silverling and next to Granberg. The latter of whom was staring at him.

"Hope you came to lose, Newsie!" Eversley called out from beside Silverling.

"Well, I came with money. Not sure how much losing I will be doing. I'm pretty good at cards."

Everyone at the table laughed as he was dealt into the next hand after a quick exchange of money for poker chips and a full glass of beer. It would have been any night at any bar on Earth. The cards came quick enough, and as his turn came, he took a quick peek: a ten of hearts and two of clubs.

"Think I'm going to need more booze," he muttered. to himself and Granberg, who grunted in response.

Gamma Squadron will deploy again, in the Avalon Assignment

Don't miss out!

Visit the website below and you can sign up to receive emails whenever E.L. Grover publishes a new book. There's no charge and no obligation.

https://books2read.com/r/B-A-BWMV-BXDCC

BOOKS 2 READ

Connecting independent readers to independent writers.